Twice Loved

WANDA E.
BRUNSTETTER

BARBOUR
PUBLISHING

Published by Barbour Publishing, Inc., P.O. Box 719, Uhrichsville,
Ohio 44683, www.barbourbooks.com

*Our mission is to publish and distribute inspirational products offering
exceptional value and biblical encouragement to the masses.*

 Member of the
Evangelical Christian
Publishers Association

Printed in the United States of America

Introduction

Japan's unconditional surrender to the Allies on September 2, 1945, ended World War II. America and her allies rejoiced. The idea of peace had never seemed more precious than to those who had given faithful service on the home front, as well as those who had served on the battlefield.

Yet much needed to be done before peace could be achieved. Those who had lost loved ones grieved. Families of those who were classified as prisoners of war or missing in action hoped and prayed for the day when their loved ones might return home. Factories that had been engaged in the production of war materials returned to their former pursuits. Thousands of "Rosie the Riveters," women who had replaced men who had been called to defend their country, were no longer needed. Returning military personnel further flooded the job market.

There was rejoicing and mourning, newly created problems, and the adjustment from war to peace, but the spark of hope that had kept people through the dark days of war, rationing, and personal sacrifice burned high. A weary world looked forward to a season of peace on earth, goodwill to men.

Prologue

Dan Fisher went down on his knees in front of the sofa where his wife lay. Darcy had been diagnosed with leukemia several months earlier, and short of a miracle, he knew she wouldn't have long to live.

"I'm almost finished with this quilt," Darcy murmured, lifting one corner of the colorful patchwork covering she had been working on since she'd first gotten sick. It was made from various shapes of cotton and velveteen material, in shades of blue, scarlet, gold, and green, and had been hand tied. She'd been able to do much of the stitching while lying in bed

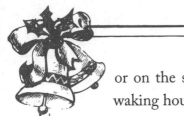

or on the sofa, where she spent most of her waking hours.

Dan nodded. "It's beautiful, honey—just like you."

"I want you to have it as a remembrance of me." Tears gathered in the corners of Darcy's dark brown eyes, and she blinked them away. "It will bring you solace after I'm gone and help you remember to comfort others in need."

Unable to voice his thoughts, Dan reached for Darcy's hand. When she squeezed his fingers, he was amazed at the strength of her touch.

"There are things we must discuss," she whispered.

Dan nodded, wishing they could talk about anything other than his wife's imminent death.

"Please promise you'll keep Twice Loved open."

Dan knew how important Darcy's used-toy store was to her and to all the children she had ministered to by providing inexpensive or free toys. Little ones whose fathers were away at war and those who'd been left with only one parent had received a

measure of happiness, thanks to Darcy and her special store.

"I'll keep the place going," he promised. "Whenever I look at this quilt, I'll remember the labor of love that went into making it, and I'll do my best to help others in need."

Chapter 1

September 1945

Bev Winters shut her desk drawer with such force that the cherished picture of her late husband toppled to the floor. Her hands shook as she bent to retrieve it, but she breathed a sigh of relief to see that the glass was intact and Fred's handsome face smiled back at her.

Joy Lundy poked her head around the partition that separated her and Bev's work spaces in the accounting department at Bethlehem Steel. "What happened, Bev? I heard a crash."

Bev clutched the picture to her chest and sank

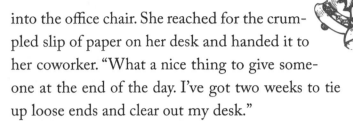

into the office chair. She reached for the crumpled slip of paper on her desk and handed it to her coworker. "What a nice thing to give someone at the end of the day. I've got two weeks to tie up loose ends and clear out my desk."

Joy scanned the memo, her forehead creasing as she frowned. "I heard there would be some cutbacks, now that the war is over and many of our returning men will need their old jobs back. I just didn't realize it would be so soon—or that you'd be one of those they let go."

Bev pulled the bottom drawer open and scooped up her pocketbook. "It's probably for the best," she mumbled. "I was thinking I might have to look for another job anyway."

"You were? How come?"

Bev hung her head, feeling the humiliation of what had transpired yesterday afternoon.

Joy touched Bev's trembling shoulder. "Tell me what's wrong."

"I—I—It's nothing, really." Bev was afraid to admit that their boss had tried to take advantage of her. What if Joy told someone and the news spread around the building? Bev's reputation could be tarnished, and so would her Christian testimony. Here at Bethlehem Steel she'd tried to tell others about Christ through her actions and by inviting them to attend church. No, it would be best if she kept quiet about what had happened with Frank Martin. She'd be leaving in two weeks anyway.

Joy tapped Bev gently on the shoulder, driving her disconcerting thoughts to the back of her mind. "I'm here if you want to talk."

Bev nodded, as tears clouded her vision. "I–I'd better get going. I don't want to be late picking Amy up at the sitter's."

Joy returned to her own desk, and Bev left the office. Bev had only taken a few steps when she bumped into a tall man with sandy-blond hair. She didn't recognize him and figured he must not work here or could be a returning veteran— perhaps the one who would be taking her book-keeping position.

When the man looked down, Bev noticed that

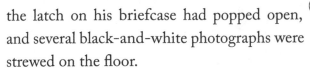

the latch on his briefcase had popped open, and several black-and-white photographs were strewed on the floor.

"I'm so sorry," she apologized.

"It's my fault. I wasn't watching where I was going." He squatted down and began to collect the pictures. "I'm here to do a photo shoot for management and can't find the conference room. Do you know where it is?"

"Two doors down. Here, let me help you with those." Bev knelt on the floor, unmindful of her hose that already had a small tear in them. As she helped gather the remaining photos, she almost collided with the man's head.

For a few seconds, he stared at Bev with a look of sympathy. Could he tell she'd been crying? Did he think she was clumsy for bumping into him, causing his briefcase to open?

She handed the man his photos and stood, smoothing her dark green, knee-length skirt. "Sorry about the pictures. I hope none of them are ruined."

He put the photos back into his briefcase,

snapped it closed, and rose. "No harm done. Thanks for your help."

"You're welcome."

The man hesitated a moment, like he wanted to say something more, but then he strode down the hallway toward the conference room.

Bev headed in the opposite direction, anxious to get her daughter and head for home.

As Dan strolled down the hallway, he thought about the young woman he'd bumped into a few minutes ago. She wore her dark hair in a neat pageboy and had the bluest eyes he'd ever seen. If he wasn't mistaken, there'd been tears in her eyes, and he figured she must have been crying before they collided.

It's none of my business, he admonished himself. *My desire to help others sometimes clouds my judgment.*

Dan spotted the conference room and was about to open the door, when a middle-aged man with a balding head stopped him. "Hey, aren't you Dan Fisher?"

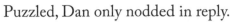

Puzzled, Dan only nodded in reply.

"I'm Pete Mackey. We met back in '39 when we were photographing the pedestrian suspension bridge that links Warren and Valley Streets. That was shortly after it was damaged by a severe storm."

"I remember. That was quite a mess," Dan said. "The new bridge is holding together nicely though."

"Yeah, until the next hurricane hits the coast."

"I hope not."

Pete's pale eyebrows drew together. "Say, didn't you lose your wife a few years ago? I remember reading her obituary in the newspaper."

"Darcy died of leukemia in the fall of '43." Dan's skin prickled. He hated to think about how he'd lost his precious wife, much less discuss his feelings with a near stranger.

"That must have been rough."

"It was."

"Do you have any children?"

"No, but we wanted some."

"Me and the wife have five." Pete gave his left

earlobe a couple of pulls. "Kids can be a handful at times, but I wouldn't trade mine for anything."

Dan smiled and glanced at his watch. In about two minutes he would be late for his appointment.

"You here on business?" Pete asked.

"Yes. I've been asked to photograph some of the managers. How about you?"

"Came to interview a couple of women who lost their husbands in the war."

"I see. Well it was nice seeing you again." Dan turned toward the door, hoping Pete would take the hint and be on his way.

"Say, I was wondering if you could do me a favor," Pete said.

Dan glanced over his shoulder. "What's that?"

"I'm working for *Family Life Magazine* now, and I've been asked to write an article on how people deal with grief. Since you lost your wife, I figured you might be able to give me some helpful insights."

Dan pivoted on his heel. "Are you suggesting an interview?"

"Yep. I'm sure the article will reach people all over the country who lost a loved one during the war. Some might be helped by your comments or advice, same as with the folks I'll be interviewing here today."

Dan's face warmed, and his palms grew sweaty. Even though it had been two years since Darcy's death, it was still difficult to talk about. Hardly a day had gone by that he hadn't yearned for her touch. He wasn't ready to share his feelings—not even to help someone going through grief.

"Sorry," Dan mumbled. "I'm not interested in being interviewed for your magazine, and I'm late for an appointment." He hurried off before Pete could say anything more.

Chapter 2

Dan leaned against his polished oak office chair and raked his fingers through the back of his hair, preparing to look over some proofs from a recent wedding he'd done. Things had been busy lately, and soon would get even busier, with Christmas only three months away. Many people wanted portraits taken to give as gifts, and he hoped those who did wouldn't wait until the last minute to schedule an appointment. That had happened in the past, and there were days when he wondered why he'd ever become a photographer.

Dan thought about his first career choice and

how he had wanted to join the navy shortly after he got out of high school. However, due to a knee injury he'd received playing football, he had been turned down for active duty.

Guess it's just as well, he thought. *If I'd gone into the navy, I might never have met Darcy. Might not be alive today either.*

He thought about the radio broadcasts he'd listened to during the war, and the newspaper articles that had given accounts of the battles, often mentioning those in the area who'd lost their lives in the line of duty. War was an ugly thing, but he knew it was a price that sometimes had to be paid in order to have freedom.

Dan's thoughts were halted when the telephone rang. Knowing it could be a client, he reached for the receiver. "Fisher's Photography Studio. Dan speaking."

"Hi, Danny. How are you this evening?" The lilting voice on the other end of the line purred like a kitten, and he recognized it immediately.

"I'm fine, Leona. How are you?"

"Okay." There was a brief pause. "You said you enjoyed my spaghetti and meatballs last week when you came over for supper, so I was hoping you'd join me tonight for my meat loaf special."

"I appreciate the offer, but I'm busy right now, Leona."

Dan's next-door neighbor's placating voice suddenly turned to ice. "I hope you're not giving me the brush-off."

"Of course not. I've got work to do in the studio, and I'll be here until quite late."

"I'm really disappointed, Danny."

Dan clenched the phone cord between his fingers. Leona Howard was a nice enough woman, but why did she have to be so pushy? "Can I take a rain check?" he asked.

"Okay, but I plan to collect on that rain check soon."

"I'd better get back to work, so I'll talk to you later. Good-bye, Leona." Dan hung up the phone with a sense of relief. He didn't want to hurt the woman's feelings, but they weren't right for each other. At least, she wasn't right for him. Leona was nothing like Darcy. In fact, she was the exact opposite of her. Leona usually wore her platinum-blond hair in one of those wavy updos, with her bangs swept to one side. Darcy's chestnut-brown hair had been shoulder length and worn in a soft pageboy. Leona plastered on enough makeup to sink a battleship, and Darcy had worn hardly any at all.

Dan massaged his forehead, making little circles with the tips of his fingers. *Who am I kidding? I'm not ready to commit to another woman, and I may never be. Besides, Leona is not a Christian, and that fact alone would keep me from becoming seriously involved with her.*

A couple of times, when Leona first started inviting him to her house for a meal, Dan had asked her to attend church with him. She'd flatly refused, saying church was for weak people who needed a crutch. Leona wasn't weak, and she'd proved that when her husband was killed on the USS *Arizona* during the bombing of Pearl Harbor. Leona had become a nurse and picked up the pieces of her life so well that it made Dan wonder if she'd ever loved her husband at all.

A rumble in the pit of Dan's stomach reminded him that it was nearly suppertime. He momentarily fought the urge to call his wife on the phone and ask what she was fixing tonight. He glanced through the open door of his office, leading to the used-toy store on the other side of the building. There was Darcy's quilt hanging over the wooden rack he'd made. The coverlet was a reminder of her undying love and brought him some measure of comfort.

Bev sank into a chair at the kitchen table and opened the newspaper. Yesterday had been her last day at Bethlehem Steel, and she hoped to find something else right away. She *needed* to, as the meager savings she'd put away wouldn't last long.

She scanned the HELP WANTED section but soon realized there were no bookkeeping jobs available. "They've probably all been taken by returning war veterans," she grumbled.

Her conscience pricked, and she bowed her head. "Forgive me, Lord. I'm thankful that so many of our soldiers have come home. I only wish Fred could have been one of them."

Tears stung Bev's eyes as she thought about the way her husband had been killed, along with thousands of other men and women who'd been at Pearl Harbor on December 7, 1941. For nearly four years now, Bev had been without Fred, but at least she'd had a job.

She returned her attention to the newspaper. Surely there had to be something she could do. She was about to give up and start supper when she noticed an ad she hadn't seen before.

Wanted: Reliable person to manage used-toy store. Must have good people skills and be able to balance the books. If interested, apply at Twice Loved, on the corner of North Main and Tenth Street, Easton, Pennsylvania.

She pursed her lips. "Maybe I should drop by there tomorrow after I take Amy to school. Even if I don't get the job, I might be able to find an inexpensive doll or stuffed animal I could put away for her Christmas present."

As if on cue, Bev's six-year-old daughter burst into the room. Her blue eyes brimmed with tears, and her chin trembled like a leaf caught in a breeze.

Bev reached out and pulled Amy into her arms. "What's wrong, honey?"

"I was playin' with Baby Sue, and her head fell off."

"Why don't you go get the doll, and I'll see if I can put her back together."

Amy shook her head as more tears came. "Her neck's tore. The head won't stay on."

Bev knew enough about rubber dolls to realize that once the body gave way, there was little that could be done except to buy a new doll.

Her gaze came to rest on the newspaper ad again. *I really do need to pay a visit to Twice Loved.*

Chapter 3

B ev stood in front of Twice Loved, studying the window display. There were several stuffed animals leaning against a stack of books, a toy fire truck, two cloth dolls, and a huge teddy bear with a red ribbon tied around its neck. Propped against the bear's feet was a sign that read: HELP WANTED. INQUIRE WITHIN.

Bev drew in a deep breath and pushed open the door. Inside, there was no one in sight, so she made her way to the wooden counter in the center of the room. A small bell sat on one end, and she gave it a jingle. A few minutes later, a door at the back of the store opened, and a man stepped out.

Her heart did a little flip-flop. He was tall with sandy-blond hair and wore a pair of tan slacks and a long-sleeved white shirt rolled up to the elbows.

Bev recognized him—but from where? She'd never been in this store before. She was tempted to ask if they'd met somewhere, but that might seem too forward.

The man stepped up beside her. "May I help you?"

Bev moistened her lips, feeling as though her tongue were tied in knots. "I—um—do you have any dolls?"

He smiled and made a sweeping gesture with his hand. "All over the store, plus toys of all sorts."

"I'm looking for something inexpensive that's in good condition."

"Shouldn't be a problem. Most of the toys are in pretty fair shape."

"Would you mind if I have a look around?"

"Help yourself." He stepped aside, and Bev walked slowly around the room until she came to a basket full of dolls. Surely there had to be something here Amy would like. And if they weren't too expensive, maybe she could buy two—one to replace Amy's Baby Sue, and the other for Amy's Christmas present.

Bev knelt in front of the basket and riffled through the dolls. A few minutes later, the man pulled up a short wooden stool and plunked down beside her. "Have we met before? You look familiar."

She felt the heat of a blush creep up the back of her neck. "I'm. . .uh. . .not sure. You look familiar to me, too."

They stared at one another a few seconds, and his scrutiny made Bev's cheeks grow even warmer. Suddenly she remembered where she'd seen the man. It was at Bethlehem Steel, the day she'd rushed into the hallway in tears after receiving her layoff notice. She had been mortified when she bumped the man's briefcase and it opened, spilling his photographs. But no, this couldn't be the same man. The man she'd met was obviously a photographer, not a used-toy salesman.

"I'm Dan Fisher, and I have a photography studio in the back of this building," he said, reaching out his hand.

"I'm Bev Winters." She was surprised by the firm yet gentle handshake he gave. "You're a photographer, not the owner of Twice Loved?"

"I do both. The used-toy store was my wife's business, and I took it over after she died two years ago from leukemia."

"I'm sorry for your loss." Bev's heart went out to Dan. It was plain to see from the way his hazel-colored eyes clouded over that he still missed his wife. She could understand that, for she missed Fred, too.

"Were you at Bethlehem Steel a few weeks ago?" she questioned.

He nodded. "I was asked to take some pictures for management, and—" Suddenly his face broke into a smile. "Say, you're that woman I bumped into, aren't you?"

"Actually, I think I bumped your briefcase."

"Ever since you came into the store, I've been trying to place you."

"Same here."

He motioned to the basket of dolls. "What kind of doll are you looking for?"

"I might buy two. One needs to be a baby doll, because my daughter's favorite doll is broken beyond repair. I'd also like to find something to give her for Christmas."

"How about this?" he said, pointing to a pretty doll with a bisque head.

Beth looked at the price tag and released a sigh. "I'm sure Amy would like it, but I can't afford that much right now." She plucked a baby doll from the basket. Its head was made from compressed wood, and the body was cloth. "I think this could replace Amy's rubber doll. How much is it? I don't see a price sticker."

"Some of the dolls in that basket came in last week, and I haven't had a chance to price them yet. How does twenty-five cents sound?"

Her mouth fell open. "You can't be serious. The doll probably cost at least three dollars when it was new."

He shrugged. "Maybe so, but it's used now, and

twenty-five cents seems fair to me."

Bev sat a few seconds, thinking about his offer and trying to decide how best to reply. *I shouldn't have told him I couldn't afford the other doll. He probably feels sorry for me or thinks I'm a charity case.* She pinched the bridge of her nose, hoping to release some of the tension she felt. "Maybe I'll take this doll now. If I find a job soon, I might be able to purchase the bisque doll later."

His eyebrows lifted in obvious surprise. "You're not working at Bethlehem Steel any longer?"

She shook her head. "I was laid off. A returning soldier used to have my bookkeeping position."

"I'm sorry." The compassion Bev saw in Dan's eyes made her want to cry, but she couldn't. It would be humiliating to break down in front of someone she barely knew.

"I understand that a lot of women who were filling job slots during the war are now out of work," he commented.

"Which would be fine if my husband were coming home."

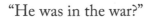

"He was in the war?"

She nodded, willing her tears not to spill over. "Fred was killed during the Pearl Harbor attack. He was aboard the USS *Maryland*."

"I'm sorry," Dan said again. He reached out his hand as though he might touch her, but quickly withdrew it and offered Bev a crooked grin instead.

She felt relief. One little sympathetic gesture and she might give in to her threatening tears.

"An elderly lady from church worked here part-time for a while," Dan said, as though needing to change the subject. "Alma fell and broke her hip a few weeks ago, so she had to quit. I've been trying to run both Darcy's toy store and my photo business ever since. It's become an almost impossible task, so I'm looking for someone to manage Twice Loved." He released a puff of air. "You think you might be interested in the job?"

Interested? Of course she was interested. That was one of the reasons she'd come here today. "I did notice your HELP WANTED sign in the window," Bev admitted.

"I put it there yesterday. Also placed an ad in the newspaper."

"I read that ad in last night's paper," Bev said, feeling the need to be completely honest with him.

"You did?"

"Yes, but that's not the only reason I came here this morning. I really do need a doll for my daughter."

"I appreciate your truthfulness," he said smiling. "I'm a Christian, and I believe honesty and integrity are important—especially where business matters are concerned."

"I'm a Christian, too." Bev fingered the lace edge on the baby doll's white nightgown. "I would have told you right away that I was interested in the job, but I was taken by surprise when you stepped into the room and I couldn't figure out where we had met."

He chuckled.

"So, about the position here. . .what hours would I be expected to work, and what would the job entail?"

"The store's closed on Sundays and Mondays, so

I'd need you to work Tuesday through Saturday from nine to five. Could you manage that?"

Bev nibbled on the inside of her cheek as a sense of apprehension crept up her spine. Would he refuse to hire her if he knew she couldn't work Saturdays?

"Is there a problem?" he asked. "I sense some hesitation."

"The woman who watches my little girl after school is not available on weekends, so it would be difficult for me to work on Saturdays."

Dan shrugged. "That's not a problem. Bring your daughter to the store."

"You wouldn't mind?"

"Not at all. I have no children of my own, but I like kids." He shrugged. "Besides, a lot of kids come here with their folks. Maybe your daughter could keep them occupied while their parents shop. In between customers she can play with the toys."

Bev could hardly believe the man was so accommodating. Her boss at Bethlehem Steel would never have considered such a thing. Of course, there weren't a bunch of toys available there.

"What type of work would be expected of me?" she asked.

"Keeping the books, waiting on customers, going through boxes of toys that have been donated—that sort of thing."

"I think I could handle it." She felt her face heat up again. "That is, if you're willing to give me a try."

Dan stood and motioned her back to the counter. Bev followed, wondering what he had in mind.

He reached underneath, pulled out a dark green ledger, and flipped it open. "If you're a bookkeeper, you should be able to tell me if there's any hope for this store."

Bev peered at the page and frowned. The figures showed a decided lack of income, compared to the expenditures. "Why are so many of the toys given away for little or nothing?" she questioned.

"I donate a certain percentage of the proceeds from Twice Loved to children in need. It was something Darcy started before she died, and I plan to continue doing it." His forehead wrinkled.

"So many kids had to do without during wartime."

"There have been so many people affected by the war—children who have lost a parent most of all." Bev drew in a deep breath and decided to ask the question uppermost on her mind. "How can you afford to pay me if the toy store operates in the red?"

"I make enough as a photographer to cover your wages." He motioned to the ledger. "And maybe you'll figure out a way to sell more toys and put Twice Loved in the black. My only concern is whether you'll be able to handle some of the repairs."

She lifted one eyebrow in question.

"The dirty toys that come in aren't such a problem. I usually take them home and soak them in the tub. However, I'm not good with a needle and thread, the way my wife was." Dan nodded toward a colorful patchwork quilt draped over a wooden rack on the opposite wall. "Darcy finished that shortly before she died."

Bev studied the item in question, taking in the vivid colors mixed with warm hues. "It's beautiful."

"Can you sew?" he asked.

She nodded. "I don't quilt, but I can mend. I've made most of Amy's and my clothes."

"Great. I think you'll do just fine."

"Is there anything else?"

He ran his fingers through the back of his hair, sending a spicy aroma into the air that tickled Bev's nose. "You know anything about electric trains?"

Chapter 4

On her trip home, Bev sat at the back of the bus, thinking about the job. Had she made a mistake in accepting Dan Fisher's invitation to work at Twice Loved? She was sure she could handle the books, because bookkeeping was something she had been doing for the last four years. But what did she know about fixing broken dolls and stuffed animals? And a toy train, of all things!

Bev winced. Had Dan been kidding about her repairing the broken train, or did he really expect her to tackle such a job? She would have asked about it right away, but he'd received a phone call that interrupted them. When he hung up, Bev paid for the baby doll, and not wanting to miss the next bus, she had left in a hurry and forgot to ask about the broken train.

She glanced at the small box lying in her lap. Amy's new doll. The one she'd paid a quarter for. She figured it was an act of charity, but since money was tight, she'd set her independent spirit aside.

I still can't believe he suggested that I bring Amy to the store. But tomorrow's Saturday, and I can't leave her alone. I hope things will go okay during my first day on the job.

"Excuse me, but is this seat taken?"

Bev was glad for the interruption, as her worrisome thoughts were taking her nowhere. "No, you're welcome to sit here," she said to the elderly woman who stood in the aisle.

The woman slid in next to her, pushing a strand of gray hair away from her eyes. "Whew! I almost missed the bus."

"I'm glad you made it." Bev could relate to what the woman had gone through. Since Bev didn't own a car, she usually rode the bus and had dashed for it many times when she'd been late. When she worked at Bethlehem Steel, which was several miles outside of town, Bev drove to work with a coworker who owned a Hudson and lived near her apartment. With her new job being downtown, though, she would ride the bus every day.

As the bus continued on its route, Bev watched the passing scenery—the Karldon Hotel, Easton City Hall, Maxwell's Book Store. How long had it been since she'd bought a new book to read? Money was tight, and America had begun rationing things during the war. She had a feeling that despite the end of the war some things might continue to be rationed for a while.

Even though Bev had Fred's monthly veteran's pension, it was small and not enough to provide all the essentials she and Amy needed. Bev only wished her wages at Twice Loved wouldn't be coming from Dan's photography business. She hoped to find a way for the toy store to make more money and get out of the red, while keeping prices low.

Bev closed her eyes and leaned against the seat, willing herself to relax and give her troubles to the Lord. After all, He had provided her with a new job, and so quickly, too. She needed to trust Him and believe He would care for her and Amy in the days ahead.

Sometime later, Bev arrived at her apartment and was surprised to find a note taped to the door. She waited until she was inside to read it, dropping her coat and the box with the doll in it onto the couch. Then she took a seat and opened the folded paper.

Dear Mrs. Winters:

This is to inform you that due to the expected rise in heating costs this winter I need to raise your rent by five dollars a month. The increase will take effect on the fifteenth of October.

Thank you.

Sincerely,
Clyde Smithers, Manager

Bev moaned. This kind of news was not what she needed. The rent on her small two-bedroom apartment was already sixty dollars a month, and she didn't think she could afford another five. With the addition of bus fare to and from work every day, and the fact that her wages at Twice Loved wouldn't be as much as what she had made at Bethlehem Steel, she couldn't afford the rent increase.

Maybe I should look for an apartment closer to town so I can walk to work. That would save money, and perhaps I can find something cheaper to rent.

Bev dismissed that thought as quickly as it came. She had heard that apartments in the heart of the city were in demand, and with so many men and women returning from the war, it would be difficult to find one that wasn't already rented, let alone cheaper.

Bev massaged her pulsating forehead. Just when she thought the Lord was watching out for them, another problem had come along. Ever since Fred died, it seemed as if her whole world were out of control. Bev attended church on Sunday mornings, read her Bible regularly, and prayed every day. Yet her faith was beginning to waver.

Blinking back tears, she closed her eyes and prayed, "Lord, show me what to do about the increase in my rent. If there's something closer to town, please point the way."

For the last couple of hours, Dan had been sitting at his desk going over some paperwork. Trying to run two businesses by himself had put him behind in the photography studio. But that was about to change. Now that he'd hired Bev Winters to run Twice Loved, things would get back to normal. At least he hoped they would. What if Bev didn't work out? He didn't know much about the woman other than she had worked as a bookkeeper, had a young daughter, and was widowed. He hadn't thought to ask for a résumé or any references. He'd based his decision to hire Bev on her need for a job. That and the fact that she said she was a Christian.

A beautiful one at that, Dan thought, tapping his pencil along the edge of the desk. It wasn't just Bev's shiny dark hair and luminous blue eyes that attracted him either. There was something about her demeanor that reminded him of Darcy.

He rapped the side of his head with the pencil. "Get a grip on yourself. You hired the lady to run Twice Loved, not so you could become romantically involved."

The phone rang, and he grabbed for it, glad for the interruption. "Fisher's Photography. May I help you?"

"Hello, Dan. This is Pete Mackey, with *Family Life Magazine.* We talked at Bethlehem Steel a few weeks ago, remember?"

Dan's gaze went to the ceiling. "I hope you're not calling about that article you're doing on grief, because, as I told you before, I'm not interested in being interviewed."

"I'd hoped if you had a few weeks to think it over that you might have changed your mind."

"Nope. Sorry, Pete."

"Here's the phone number where I can be reached, just in case."

Dan studied a set of negatives on his desk as Pete rattled off his number. There was no point in writing it down because he had no intention of doing that interview.

"I appreciate your time," Pete said. "Please call if you ever want to talk."

"Okay, thanks. Good-bye, Pete."

Dan had no more than hung up the phone when he heard a knock on the door of his studio. *Wonder who it could be? I don't have any appointments scheduled for the rest of the day.*

When Dan opened the door, he discovered Leona Howard, holding a casserole dish wrapped in a towel with a paper sack balanced on top.

"Hi, Danny," she said, offering him a pleasant smile. "Since you've been too busy lately to have dinner at my place, I decided to bring a meal over to you this evening. It's Chicken Noodle Supreme."

Leona wore a maroon-colored, knee-length

skirt with a single-breasted jacket that had wide lapels and padded shoulders. It looked like something a woman might wear when she went out to dinner—but not to drop off a casserole for a neighbor.

"I'm working right now," Dan said as she swept into the room, her fragrant perfume leaving a trail of roses behind.

"Surely you're ready for a break. I'll be disappointed if you don't try some of my yummy casserole." Leona nodded at the paper sack. "I even brought some dishes, silverware, and napkins, so all you need to provide is a place for me to set the table."

Dan was sure the woman wasn't going to take no for an answer, so he removed the negatives and paperwork from his desk and slipped them into a folder. "You can put the food here." He pulled out his desk chair, grabbed another one for Leona, and sat down.

She quickly set out the dishes, opened the lid of the casserole dish, and served them both a hefty amount. "Oh dear, I forgot to bring something to

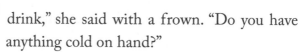

drink," she said with a frown. "Do you have anything cold on hand?"

He reached into the bottom drawer of his desk and grabbed a thermos. "It's coffee, so it's not cold."

She smiled. "That will be fine."

"Mind if I pray before we eat?"

She shrugged. "If it makes you feel better. I wasn't planning to poison you, Danny."

He bit back a chuckle. That thought had crossed his mind.

After the prayer, Dan poked his fork into the gooey mess she'd put on his plate and took a bite. Ugh! The stuff tasted worse than it looked. He grabbed his thermos, twisted the lid, and gulped down some coffee.

Leona's lower lip protruded. "You don't like it?"

Searching for words that wouldn't be a lie, Dan mumbled, "It's. . .uh. . .different." He set the thermos lid down and wiped his mouth on the cloth napkin she had provided. "I'm really not hungry."

Leona pushed her chair aside, and it nearly

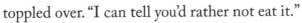

toppled over. "I can tell you'd rather not eat it."

Dan opened his mouth to reassure her, but Leona gathered her things so quickly that he barely had the presence of mind to say he was sorry.

"I'll try something different next time," she said as he followed her to the door. "Something I know you'll like."

Chapter 5

Dan took a swig of coffee and glanced at the clock on the far wall. Bev Winters should be here any minute and would be bringing her daughter along. He moved across the room and put the OPEN sign in the window. It was almost nine o'clock. Better to have the store ready for business on time, even if his new employee wasn't here yet.

I wonder if her bus was late, or maybe she had trouble getting her daughter out of bed. Sure hope I did the right thing in hiring her.

Dan thought about his favorite verses of scripture—2 Corinthians 1:3–4. It reminded him

that God is our Comforter, and because He comforts in all our troubles, we should comfort those who have trouble as well. Through God's Word and the godly counsel of his pastor, Dan had been comforted many times since Darcy's death. It was only right that he should offer comfort to Bev, who was probably hurting from the loss of her husband and also her job. He'd known yesterday that he needed to give her a chance. If hiring her to work at Twice Loved could help them both during their time of need, then so much the better.

Dan's gaze came to rest on the clock again. It was now ten minutes after nine. Bev was late. Maybe she'd changed her mind about the job and wasn't coming.

The bell above the front door jingled, and his thoughts were halted. Bev entered the store holding a metal lunch pail in one hand and a brown pocketbook in the other. A young girl stood at her side, clutching the same doll he'd sold Bev yesterday afternoon.

"I'm sorry we're late." Bev patted the sides

of her windblown hair and smoothed the wrinkles in her knee-length, navy-blue dress, covered by a short black jacket. "The bus was late, and there was more traffic this morning than I've seen in a long time."

"It's okay," Dan said with a nod. "There haven't been any customers yet." He smiled at the little girl who stood beside Bev. She was a beautiful child— curly black hair like her mother's, and the same brilliant blue eyes. She wore a beige-colored tweed coat with a pair of darkgreen overalls with patched knees peeking out from underneath. "So, this must be Amy."

"Yes." Bev's generous smile seemed to light up the room.

Darcy used to smile like that, Dan noted.

"Amy, this is Mr. Fisher, and he owns this store where I'll be working."

The child smiled shyly and glanced around the shop. "I like it here."

"Me, too." Dan's throat constricted. He and Darcy had wanted children, but that wasn't to

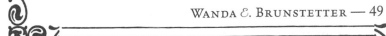

be. Did Bev Winters know how fortunate she was?

"Why don't you find a book to read?" Bev said to her daughter. "Mommy needs to begin working now."

Dan pointed across the room. "There's a table in the corner where you can sit if you want to read or work on a puzzle. Feel free to play with any of the toys that are in baskets sitting on the floor."

Amy didn't have to be asked twice. She slipped out of her coat and handed it to her mother. Then she sprinted across the room, grabbed a fat teddy bear from a wicker basket, and helped herself to a book from the bookcase. A few seconds later, she sat at the table wearing a contented grin.

Dan turned his attention back to Bev. "Should we take a look at some of the toys that need to be fixed?"

Her eyes widened. "Uh. . .about the toys. . ."

"What about them?"

"Yesterday you mentioned a broken train, and I thought I should let you know that I'm not the least bit mechanical."

He chuckled and led her over to the desk. "I was only kidding. The train will have to be sold as is."

A look of relief flooded her face. "There's an elderly man at my church who collects old trains. I could speak to him and see if he might be able to look at the broken train."

"That would be great."

Bev set her pocketbook and lunch pail on the desk, removed her jacket, and draped it and Amy's coat over the back of the wooden chair. "Which toys did you want me to see about fixing?"

"First, I'd like to tell you something."

"What's that?"

You're beautiful. Dan shook his head, hoping to clear his ridiculous thoughts. "Uh—the dress you're wearing might not be practical here at the store."

She crossed her arms. "Too dressy?"

"It's not that." Dan paused. How could he put this tactfully? "Sometimes you'll have to get down on the floor, in order to sort through the boxes of toys that come in. You'll also be working with glue

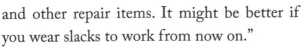

and other repair items. It might be better if you wear slacks to work from now on."

She blinked. "You wouldn't mind?"

He shook his head.

"I was expected to wear a dress at Bethlehem Steel, so I figured—"

"Wear whatever you're comfortable in here, Bev. I trust you to use good judgment."

"Thank you, Mr. Fisher."

"Dan. Please call me Dan."

Bev's cheeks turned pink as something indefinable passed between them, and she looked quickly away. "Guess you'd better show me what to do, so I can get to work."

He glanced toward the room where his studio was located. "That makes two of us."

Bev's stomach growled as her gaze went to the clock on the wall across from her. It was almost noon, and she couldn't believe how quickly the morning had passed. She'd mended two doll dresses, stitched a stuffed kitten's eyes in place, and waited on several customers. In all that time, Amy had hardly made a peep. She'd kept herself occupied with various toys, books, and puzzles. Dan excused himself soon after showing Bev what needed to be done, and he'd been in his photography studio ever since.

Should I ask him to cover for me so I can see that Amy is fed, or should I serve Amy her lunch and try to eat my sandwich while I keep an eye out for customers? Guess the latter would be better, she decided. *No point bothering Dan. He's probably busy and might not appreciate the interruption. After all, he hired me so he could be free to operate his own business and not have to run back and forth between Twice Loved and the photography studio.*

"Amy, please have a seat at the table again, and I'll bring your lunch," Bev instructed her daughter, who was now on her knees in front of a stack of wooden blocks.

"Okay, Mommy." Amy lifted her baby doll by one arm. "Can Baby Sue eat lunch with me?"

Bev smiled, pleased that the child had accepted the new doll so readily and had even given it the same name as her old doll. "Sure, sweetie. Just don't give her anything to drink, all right?"

"Okay."

A few minutes later, Amy and Baby Sue were seated in the small wooden chairs opposite each other, a peanut butter and jelly sandwich and a cup of cold milk in front of Amy.

Bev said a quick prayer, thanking God for the food, then took her bologna sandwich and the remaining milk over to the desk so she could look at the ledger while she ate. From time to time she glanced up, wondering if or when Dan might emerge from his studio. But he didn't. The only evidence that he was in the back room was the occasional ringing of his telephone.

After lunch Bev encouraged Amy to lie on a piece of carpet next to the bookcase and take a nap. Amy slept with Baby Sue tucked under one arm and a stuffed elephant under the other.

Bev decided to use this quiet time to sort through some boxes she'd found in one corner of the room. She soon discovered they were full of Christmas decorations, and it put her in the mood to decorate the store for the holidays. Perhaps it was too soon for that though. It was early October, and most of the stores didn't set out their Christmas things until sometime in November. She set the box aside, planning to ask Dan if he would mind if she decorated Twice Loved a little early. If she put some Christmas items in the store window it might attract more customers. Besides, it would help Bev get into the spirit of the holiday season. For the past several Christmases, she'd forced herself to put up a tree. Christmas wasn't the same without Fred, but for Amy's sake, Bev had gone through the motions.

Pushing the decorations aside, she turned her attention to another box. This one was full of old train cars, reminding her that she should speak to Ellis Hampton when she saw him at church tomorrow morning. She hoped he would be willing to look at the broken train. It would be cute, set up in the store window under a small, decorated tree with several dolls and stuffed animals sitting off to one side.

Bev blinked back tears as a feeling of nostalgia washed over her. Christmas used to be such a happy time, first when she was a child growing up near the Pocono Mountains, and then after she'd married Fred and they moved to Easton.

She closed her eyes and thought about their last Christmas together. She could almost smell the fragrant scent of the cedar tree they'd cut down in the woods that year. Amy was only two, and Bev remembered the touching scene as Fred carried their daughter on his shoulders while they trudged through the snow. They'd laughed and thrown snowballs, eaten the chewy brownies Bev had made, and drunk hot chocolate from the thermos she'd brought along.

Unwanted tears seeped under Bev's eyelashes and trickled down her cheeks. *Those happy days are gone for good.* Her mother and father had been killed in a car accident five years ago, and the ugly war had taken Fred away. It was hard not to feel bitter and become cynical when there were so many injustices in the world. But for Amy's sake, Beth was determined to make the best of her situation.

"Aha! I caught you sleeping on the job, didn't I?"

Bev jumped at the sound of Dan's deep voice.

"I—I wasn't sleeping." She sat up straight and swiped a hand across her damp cheeks.

"I was kidding about you taking a nap, but your daughter certainly is." Dan motioned across the room, where Amy lay curled on her side.

Bev nodded. "I suggested she rest awhile. I hope you don't mind."

"Why would I mind?"

She merely shrugged in reply. Dan didn't seem like the type to get upset over something like a child falling asleep inside his toy store. In fact, from the look on his face, Bev guessed he might be rather taken with her daughter.

Dan left the desk and headed across the room. When he reached the wooden rack where the colorful patchwork quilt was draped, he pulled it down.

Turning to give Bev a quick smile, he moved over to where Amy lay sleeping. Then he bent at the waist, covered her with the quilt, and reached out to push a wayward curl off her forehead.

The sight was so touching that Bev's heart nearly melted. She barely knew Dan, yet she could tell he had a lot of love to give. How sad that he hadn't been blessed with any children of his own.

She swallowed around the lump in her throat. Why was life so unfair? Shouldn't only good things happen to good people?

Chapter 6

On Tuesday morning Bev showed up at Twice Loved wearing an olive-green two-piece trouser suit, a pale yellow blouse, brown lace-up shoes, and the same jacket she'd worn on Saturday.

When Dan greeted her, she offered him a radiant smile. Then, as her fingers curled around the strap of her pocketbook, a little frown pinched her forehead. "I was wondering if it would be all right if I left the shop during my lunch hour today. There's an apartment for rent in the building two doors down, and I'd like the opportunity to look at it before it's taken."

"You're planning to move?"

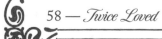

She nodded. "My rent's going up to sixty-five dollars in a few weeks, and since I live on the south side of town and have to catch the bus to get here, I thought if I could find something closer, it would be the wise thing to do."

Dan's heart went out to Bev. He could see by her troubled look that she was probably struggling financially. Many people had been faced with financial hardships during the war. "Mend and make do." That was the motto for the women in America. From the looks of the patches he'd seen on the knees of Amy's overalls the other day, Dan figured Bev had done her share of mending.

He rubbed his chin and contemplated a moment. "Maybe I can increase your wages."

Bev stared at the floor, twisting the purse strap back and forth. "Today's only my second day on the job, and I've done nothing to deserve a wage increase."

"I know, but—"

She held up her hand. "I don't need your charity, but I do need to look at that apartment today. Is it okay if I leave the store for an hour during lunch?"

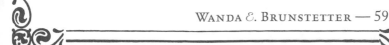

"Sure, that'll be fine." Bev was obviously a proud woman, and he really couldn't fault her for that. Maybe he could find some other way to help.

"Thank you, Dan." She pursed her lips. "Well, I'd better get busy."

"Same here. I've got some phone calls to make."

She started across the room but turned back around. "I almost forgot to ask. . . . Would you mind if I decorate the store window for Christmas a little early?"

Dan's eyebrows drew together. Other than attending the candlelight communion service at church on Christmas Eve, he hadn't done much to celebrate Christmas since Darcy died. His parents, who lived in Connecticut, had invited him to come to their place for the holidays, but Dan always turned them down, preferring to be alone.

He glanced around the store as bittersweet memories flooded over him like waves lapping against the Jersey shore. When Darcy was alive, she had decorated every nook and cranny of Twice

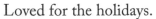

Loved for the holidays.

"If you'd rather I wait until after Thanksgiving, I understand," Bev added. "I just thought it might bring in more customers if we had the window decorated a little sooner."

Dan tapped his foot against the hardwood floor. Would it hurt if the store were decorated? It didn't mean he would have to celebrate Christmas, and it wasn't as if he would be giving up memories of Darcy by allowing Bev to do something festive here. In fact, if Darcy were alive, he knew what she would do.

"Sure, go ahead. Do whatever you'd like with the store window," he conceded.

"I'll start on the decorations when I return from my lunch break," Bev said sweetly.

"Take as long as you need to look at that apartment. I'll be praying it's the right one."

"Thanks. I appreciate that."

Bev wanted to pinch herself. Not only was the apartment she had looked at on Saturday within walking distance of Twice Loved, but the rent was five dollars cheaper than what she was paying now.

Without hesitation she had signed the lease, and she hoped that by next weekend she and Amy would be in their new home.

The move would mean Amy had to change schools, but she was young and adjusted easily. It would solve the problem of her needing a babysitter after school, too, which meant one less expense. Since the closest elementary school was only a few blocks away, Amy could walk to Twice Loved after school on the days Bev was working. Of course, she knew she would have to check with Dan first and see if he approved of the idea.

Bev smiled as she pulled out the box of Christmas decorations. Everything was working out fine. She'd been worried for nothing.

For the next hour, Bev worked on the window decorations. She had spoken to Ellis Hampton after church yesterday, and he'd agreed to look at the broken train.

She knew it was too early to get a cut tree. She

certainly didn't want it drying out and dropping needles everywhere.

For now, Bev hung several Christmas ornaments in the store window, along with some red and green bows. She also placed three dolls and a couple of stuffed animals in the center and included several small empty boxes, which were wrapped like Christmas presents.

It looks rather festive, she told herself as she stood off to one side and studied her work. She allowed herself a satisfied sigh and began humming the words to "White Christmas," swaying to the music.

"The window display looks great. Your humming's not so bad either."

Bev swiveled around. She hadn't realized Dan had come into the room and stood directly behind her. Her face flushed. "Thanks. I think it will look even better once the train is fixed and set up under a small tree." She chose not to mention her off-key music.

"Did you speak to that man from your church?" he asked, leaning against the inside casing of the window display and looking at her intently.

Bev nodded and moistened her lips. *Why do I feel so jittery whenever Dan's around?* "Ellis said he would come by sometime this afternoon," she said.

Dan smiled, but there was sadness in his hazel-colored eyes. Was he nostalgic about trains, or could something else be bothering him?

"I'll be anxious to hear what the train expert has to say." He took a few steps toward Bev but then backed away, jamming his hands into the pockets of his brown slacks. "I didn't get a chance to ask, since I was busy when you left last Saturday, but how'd things go with the apartment hunt?"

"It went well. If I can get some of the men from church to help transport my furniture, I'll be moving to my new place next Saturday. After I get off work here, of course."

"If you need the whole day to move, that won't be a problem. In fact, why don't we close the store that day, and I can help you?"

Bev noticed the look of compassion on Dan's

face. Help her move? Was there no end to this man's charitable offers?

She opened her mouth to decline, but he interrupted her. "I can't get much into my Studebaker, but I know someone who has a pickup truck. I'm pretty sure I can borrow it."

"That's nice of you, but I really couldn't accept your help." Bev appreciated his generosity, but he'd already done enough by hiring her and allowing her to bring Amy to the shop on Saturdays.

He lifted his hand and leaned forward, almost touching her lips with his fingertips, but then he quickly lowered it. "I wish you'd reconsider."

Bev swallowed around the lump in her throat. Why was it that whenever anyone was nice to her, she felt all weepy and unable to express herself? She'd been that way since Fred was killed. And why was she so determined to do things on her own? Maybe she should accept Dan's help—just this once.

"Thanks," she murmured. "I appreciate your kindness."

His ears turned pink. "Just helping a friend."

Chapter 7

Bev closed the door behind a customer and glanced around the toy store. She couldn't believe she'd been working here three weeks already. So much had happened in that time—moving, getting Amy situated in her new school, and learning more about her job. She felt she was doing fairly well, for she'd sold twice as many toys in the last few days as she had the previous week. Working at Twice Loved was proving to be fun, with not nearly as much stress as her last job. No overbearing boss making unwanted advances either.

Bev had felt such relief when Dan agreed to let

Amy come to the store after school. He even said having the child there might make some customers stay longer, since those who'd brought children along could shop at their leisure while Amy kept their little ones occupied.

There were times, like the Saturday Bev and Amy had moved, when Dan seemed so friendly and approachable. Other times he shut himself off, hiding behind the doors of his studio and barely saying more than a few words whenever he was around. Bev figured he was busy with pre-Christmas portraits, but it almost seemed as if he'd been avoiding her.

Have I done something wrong? she wondered. *Is he displeased with the way I do the books or how I run the store?*

She studied the room more closely. Everything looked neat and orderly. Cleaning and organizing was one of the first things she had done. She'd also placed some of the more interesting toys in strategic spots in order to catch the customers' attention when they entered the store. The Christmas decorations she'd put in the store window looked enticing, even though the train wasn't part of the display yet. Ellis had phoned yesterday, saying the train should be ready later this week and that he would bring it by.

Bev picked up the ledger from her desk and thumbed through the last few pages. Twice Loved was making more money than it had in several months—the profit column was proof of that.

So why did Dan seem so aloof? Was he dreading the holidays? If so, Bev couldn't blame him. This was the first year since Fred's death that she hadn't experienced anxiety about Christmas coming.

"It's probably because I'm working here among all these toys," she said aloud. "I feel like a kid again."

Bev closed the ledger and moved across the room to the sewing area. *Maybe I should invite Dan to join Amy and me for Thanksgiving dinner. It would be nice to have someone else to cook for. I could bake a small turkey, fix mashed potatoes, gravy, and stuffing. Maybe make a pumpkin and an apple pie.*

Bev took a seat at the sewing table and threaded her needle, prepared to mend the dress of the bisque doll she had chosen to give Amy for Christmas. Once the dress was repaired and the doll's wig combed and set in ringlets, she planned to put the doll in the storage closet at the back of the store until closer to Christmas. Then she would wrap it, take it home, and, when Amy wasn't looking, slip it under the tree she hoped to get for their new apartment.

Thinking of a tree caused Bev to reflect on the day they had moved. Her daughter's enthusiasm over the large living room with a tall ceiling was catching.

"We can have a giant Christmas tree, Mommy!" Amy had exclaimed. "Uncle Dan can help us decorate and climb the ladder to put the angel on top."

Bev didn't know what had prompted Amy to call Dan "Uncle," but he didn't seem to mind. In fact, the man had been patient and kind to Amy all during the move, even rocking her to sleep when she'd become tired and fussy that evening.

The bell above the door jingled, forcing Bev's thoughts aside. When Amy skipped into the room, Bev hurriedly slipped the doll's dress into a drawer.

"Mommy, Mommy, guess what?" Amy's cheeks were rosy, and she was clearly out of breath.

"What is it, sweetie?" Bev asked, bending down to help her daughter out of her wool coat.

"No, I can't take my coat off yet," Amy said, thrusting out her lower lip.

"Why not?"

" 'Cause it's snowing, and I want to play in it!"

Bev glanced out the front window. Sure enough, silvery flakes fell from the sky like twinkling diamonds. And here it was only the second week of November.

"It's beautiful," she murmured.

"Can we build a snowman?" Amy's blue eyes glistened with excitement, as she wiggled from side to side.

"Simmer down," Bev said, giving her daughter a hug. "There's not nearly enough snow yet to make

a snowball, let alone a snowman. If we had a place to build one, that is."

"We can put it out on the sidewalk in front of the store. I'll give it my hat and mittens to wear." Amy reached up to remove her stocking cap, but Bev stopped her.

"Whoa! You need your hat and mittens—you would get cold without them."

"What about the snowman? Won't he get cold without anything on his head or hands?"

Bev chuckled. "Oh Amy, I don't think—"

"What's all this about a snowman?"

Both Bev and Amy turned at the sound of Dan's deep voice. Then Amy darted across the room and grabbed hold of his hand. "It's snowing, Uncle Dan! Can we build a snowman?"

"Amy, I just told you there's not enough snow," Bev reminded her. "Besides, Uncle Dan—I mean, Mr. Fisher—is busy and doesn't have time to play in the snow."

Dan shook his head and gave Amy's hand a squeeze. "Who says I'm too busy to have a little fun?"

"Yippee!" Amy shouted.

Bev took a few steps toward him. "Do you really have the time for this?"

"For Amy and fun in the snow—absolutely!" His face sobered, and he bent down so he was eye level with the child. "There's not enough snow to build a snowman, but we can run up and down the sidewalk and catch snowflakes on our tongue." He glanced over at Bev and smiled. "How about it, Mommy? Why don't you slip into your coat and join us?"

She laughed self-consciously. "Oh, I couldn't do that."

"Why not?"

She made a sweeping gesture with her hand. "Who would mind the store?"

Dan tweaked Amy's nose and gave Bev a quick wink. "Let the store mind itself, because I think we all deserve some fun!"

Dan couldn't remember when he'd felt so exuberant or enjoyed himself so much. Certainly not since

Darcy had taken ill.

For the last half hour, the three of them had been running up and down the sidewalk, slipping and sliding in the icy snow, catching snowflakes on their tongues, and singing Christmas carols at the top of their lungs. Some folks who passed by joined in their song. Some merely smiled and kept on walking. A few unfriendly faces shook their heads and mumbled something about it not being Christmas yet. One elderly woman glared at Dan and said, "Some people never grow up."

Dan didn't care what anyone thought. He'd been cooped up in his studio for several days and needed the fresh air. He drew in a deep breath, taking in a few snowflakes in the process. *If I had known this was going to feel so good, I would have done it sooner.*

The sidewalk was covered with a good inch of snow now, and feeling like a mischievous boy, Dan bent down and scooped up a handful of the powdery stuff. He then trotted up the sidewalk, grabbed hold of Bev's collar, and dropped the snow down the back of her coat.

She shrieked and whirled around. "Hey! That was cold!"

"Of course it's cold. Snow's always cold." Dan winked at Amy, and she snickered.

"Stop that, or I won't invite you to join Amy and me for Thanksgiving." Bev wrinkled her nose. "That is, if you have no other plans."

He grinned. "I have no plans, and I'd be happy to have dinner at your place."

Bev smiled, and Amy clapped her hands.

"Can I bring anything?"

She shook her head. "Just a hearty appetite."

Before Dan could respond, two teenage girls strode up to them. Each held several wreaths in their hands. Dan recognized them and realized they attended his church.

"Hi, Mr. Fisher," Dorothy said. "Looks like you're havin' some fun today."

"Sure am," he replied with a grin.

"We came by to see if you'd like to buy a wreath for your front door," Amber put in.

He glanced at Bev. "Might be nice to have one

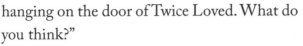

hanging on the door of Twice Loved. What do you think?"

She nodded. "Sounds good to me."

Dorothy moved toward Bev. "Would you like to buy one to take home?"

"Thanks anyway, but it will be all I can do to afford a tree."

Dan was tempted to give Bev the money for a wreath, but he figured she would see it as charity. She'd made it clear that she didn't want his help and was making it difficult for him to do anything nice for her and Amy. So he kept quiet and paid the girls for one wreath then went to hang it on the door of Twice Loved.

Just as the teens were leaving, an elderly couple showed up, wanting to buy something in the store.

"I'd better get back inside," Bev said, hurrying past Dan.

He nodded. "Amy and I will be there in a minute."

Bev and the couple entered the store, and Dan reached for Amy's hand. "How would you like to

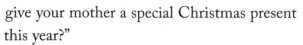

give your mother a special Christmas present this year?"

She grinned up at him with snowflakes melting on her dark, curly lashes. "What is it?"

"Can you keep a secret?"

She bobbed her head up and down.

"Let's go inside my photography studio, and I'll tell you about it."

Chapter 8

I'm sorry, Leona," Dan said into the phone, "but I can't come to your place for Thanksgiving."

"Why not?"

"Because I've made other plans."

There was a long pause, and he could almost see Leona's furrowed brows.

"Are you going to spend the holiday with your folks this year?"

"No. I'll be staying in town."

"But you're having dinner with someone?"

Dan tapped his fingers along the edge of his desk, anxious to end this conversation. He still had some book work to do, and another photo shoot was scheduled in half an hour. "I've been invited to eat with Bev Winters and her daughter, Amy."

"Bev Winters? Who's she?" Leona's voice sounded strained, and Dan had a hunch she might be jealous. Of course, she had no right to be. He'd never given her any hope that he was interested in starting a relationship. Besides, Bev was an employee, not his girlfriend.

"Danny, are you still there?"

"Yes, Leona, although I do need to hang up. I've got a client coming soon."

"First tell me who this *Bev* person is."

"She's the woman I hired to run Twice Loved."

Leona made no reply.

"I really do need to go. Thanks for the invite."

Leona sighed. "Have a nice holiday, and I'll see you soon." She hung up the phone before he could say good-bye.

Dan massaged his forehead, feeling a headache coming on. He reached for his cup of lukewarm coffee and gulped some down as the picture of Darcy hanging on the far wall caught his attention. Even though it had been two years since her death, he still loved her and probably always would.

Bev had been scurrying around her apartment all morning, checking the turkey in the oven, dusting furniture, sweeping floors, setting the table, and preparing the rest of the meal. Amy was in the living room with her new coloring book and crayons. Last week, shortly after their romp in the snow, Bev had seen her daughter go into Dan's studio. When Amy emerged a short time later, she had a box of crayons and a coloring book, which she said were a gift from Dan. He really was a nice man.

Bev glanced at the clock on the far wall. It was one thirty. Dan should be here soon, and she still needed to change clothes and put on some makeup.

"I'll be in the bedroom getting ready!" Bev called to Amy. "If anyone knocks on the door, don't answer it. Come and get me, okay?"

"All right, Mommy."

A short time later, Bev stood in front of the small mirror hanging above her dresser. She'd chosen a dusty-pink rayon-crepe dress with inset sleeves to wear. It was homemade and last year's style, but she felt it looked presentable.

When Bev reached into her top dresser drawer for a pair of hose, she discovered that her one and only pair had a run in one leg that went all the way from the heel up to the top.

"I can't wear this," she muttered. "Maybe I should draw a line down the back of my leg, like I've seen some women do when they have no hosiery."

Bev rummaged around in her drawer until she found a dark brown eyebrow pencil. Craning her neck, she stretched her left leg behind her and bent backward. Beginning at the heel of her foot, she drew a line up past her knee and then did the same to the other leg. "That will have to do," she grumbled, wishing she had a full-length mirror so she could see how it looked.

A knock at the door let Bev know Dan had

arrived. She clicked off the light and left the bedroom. When Bev opened the front door, she was surprised to see a wreath hanging there.

Dan smiled at her. "Happy Thanksgiving."

"Same to you." She pointed to the wreath. "This is pretty, but I told you not to bring anything except your appetite."

He shrugged and turned his hands palm up. "It was there when I got here."

Bev squinted at the item in question. It hadn't been there this morning when she'd gone next door to borrow a cup of flour to make gravy.

"Looks like a mystery Santa Claus paid you a visit," Dan said with a chuckle.

Bev had no idea who it could be, but the pretty wreath with a red bow did look festive, so she decided not to worry about who the donor was. She opened the door wider. "Please come inside."

Dan sniffed the air as he entered Bev's apartment. "Umm. . .something sure smells good."

Bev nodded toward the kitchen. "That would be the turkey. Would you mind carving it for me?"

"I'd be happy to."

"Follow me."

Dan stopped at the living room to say hello to Amy, and then he caught up to Bev. When she'd opened the door to let him in, he had noticed how pretty she looked in her frilly pink dress. He hadn't seen the backs of her legs then, but now, as she led the way to the kitchen, Dan couldn't help but notice the strange, squiggly dark lines running up both legs.

"What happened, Bev?" he queried. "Did Amy use her new crayons to draw on your legs?"

Bev whirled around, her face turning as pink as her dress. "I—I didn't have a decent pair of hose to wear, so I improvised."

Dan tried to keep a straight face, but he couldn't hold back the laughter bubbling in his throat.

Bev's eyes pooled with tears, and he realized he had embarrassed her. "I'm sorry. If you'd told me you needed new hosiery, I would have given you the money."

She lifted her chin. "I don't need your money or your pity, and I'm sorry you think my predicament is so funny."

"I don't really." He glanced at the crooked lines again and fought the temptation to gather her into his arms.

Bev craned her neck and stuck one leg out behind her. When she looked back at him, she wore a half smile. Soon the smile turned into a snicker. The snicker became a giggle, and the giggle turned into a chortle. She covered her mouth with the palm of her hand and stared up at him. "You had every right to laugh. What I did was pretty silly. But I was worried that if I didn't wear any hose, you'd think I wasn't properly dressed."

Dan shook his head. "I'd never think that, and as far as your being worried. . .I have a little quote about worry hanging in my studio."

"What does it say?"

" 'Worry is the darkroom in which negatives can develop.' "

She pursed her lips. "Your point is well taken. I do have a tendency to worry."

He wiggled his eyebrows. "Still want me to carve that bird?"

"Absolutely." She turned toward the door leading to the hallway. "While you do, I think I'll change into a comfortable pair of slacks."

"Good idea." Dan winked at Bev, and she scurried out of the room.

The rest of the afternoon went well, and Bev felt more relaxed wearing a pair of tan slacks and a cream-colored blouse than she had in the dress. After they'd stuffed themselves on turkey and all the trimmings, Bev, Dan, and Amy played a game of dominoes in the living room.

Soon Amy fell asleep, and Dan carried the child to her room. When he returned a few minutes later, he took a seat on the sofa beside Bev. She handed him a cup of coffee and placed two pieces of apple pie on the coffee table in front of them. It was pleasant sitting here with him. Bev hadn't felt this comfortable with a man since Fred was alive. Dan seemed so kind and compassionate, and he was a lot of fun. If she were looking for love and romance, it would be easy to fall for a man like him.

She glanced at Dan out of the corner of her eye. Was he experiencing the same feelings toward her? Had he enjoyed the day as much as she had?

As if he could read her thoughts, Dan reached over and took Bev's hand. "Thanks for inviting me today. I had a nice time, and the meal was delicious."

"You're welcome. I'm glad you came."

"I'd like to reciprocate," he said. "Would you and Amy go out to dinner with me some night next week?"

Bev moistened her lips, not sure how to respond. If she agreed to go to dinner, would that mean they were dating?

Of course not, silly. He just wants to say thank you for today.

Bev leaned over and handed Dan his plate of apple pie. "A meal out sounds nice, but you're not obligated to—"

"I know that, Bev." He forked a piece of pie into his mouth. "Yum. Apple's my favorite."

"Thanks. My grandmother gave me the recipe."

They sat in companionable silence as they drank their coffee and ate the pie. When Dan finished, he set the empty plate and cup on the coffee table and stood. "Guess I should be going."

"Amy will be disappointed when she wakes up and finds you are gone."

He reached for his coat, which he'd placed on the back of a chair when he first arrived. "Tell your daughter I'll see her bright and early tomorrow. Since she has no school until Monday, you'll be bringing her to work with you, right?"

Bev nodded. "The day after Thanksgiving should be a busy time at the store."

"Which is why I plan to give you a hand, at least for part of the day."

"I appreciate that." Bev walked Dan to the door, and when she opened it, he hesitated. She thought he might want to say something more, but he merely smiled and strolled into the hallway. "See you tomorrow, Bev."

Chapter 9

Bev plugged in the lights on the small Christmas tree she and Amy had picked out this morning for Twice Loved, after Dan had given her some money to purchase it. Amy could decorate the tree with silver tinsel and shiny red glass balls, while Bev waited on customers.

The decorations would look even better if the toy train were here, Bev thought as she scrutinized the window display. *I wonder why Ellis hasn't come by yet. He was supposed to have it ready last week. If he doesn't show up soon, I may give him a call.*

"Isn't the tree pretty?" Amy asked, pulling Bev's thoughts aside.

"Yes, it's very nice. Now be sure to drape the strands of tinsel neatly over the branches," Bev said as Amy dove into the box of decorations.

"I will."

The bell on the front door jingled, and Bev turned her head to see who had entered the store.

A young woman with platinum-blond hair piled high on her head swept through the door holding a cardboard box in her hands. She wore a black wool coat with a fur collar, and a blue, knee-length skirt peeked out from underneath. The woman stood there a few seconds, fluttering her long lashes, as she glanced around the room.

"May I help you?" Bev asked.

"I came to see Danny. Is he here?"

Bev motioned toward the back room. "He's in his studio, but I believe he plans to work in the toy store later today. May I give him a message?"

The woman stared at Bev with a critical eye, and it made Bev feel uncomfortable. "Are you the person

he hired to run Twice Loved?"

Bev nodded. "I'm Bev Winters. Are you a friend of Dan's, or are you here looking for a used toy?"

"My name's Leona Howard. I'm Danny's neighbor and a good friend." She tapped her long red fingernails along the edge of the box. "I have no need for used toys, but I would like you to tell Danny I'm here and wish to speak with him."

Bev glanced at the back room again. "I believe he's on the phone, and I would hate to interrupt him. So if you'd like to wait—"

"Fine. I'll get him myself." Leona pushed past Bev, bumping her arm with the box.

"I—I really don't think—"

"Just go back to whatever you were doing!" Leona called over her shoulder.

Bev stood there dumbfounded as the brazen woman entered Dan's studio without even knocking. Then with a shrug, she took a seat at the desk, knowing she needed to make price stickers for some newly donated stuffed animals and get them set out.

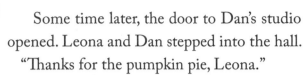

Some time later, the door to Dan's studio opened. Leona and Dan stepped into the hall.

"Thanks for the pumpkin pie, Leona."

"Now don't forget that rain check you promised me, Danny," Leona said sweetly. "How about one night next week?"

Bev put her head down and forced herself to focus on the project before her. It wasn't her nature to eavesdrop, but it was hard to think about anything other than Dan and his lady friend. She glanced up once, and it was just in time to see Leona kiss Dan on the cheek. He grinned kind of self-consciously, and his ears turned red.

That's what you get for thinking you might have a chance with Dan, Bev fumed. Was that what she believed? Could she and Dan have a relationship that went beyond boss to employee, or friend to friend? Probably not, if he was dating his flamboyant neighbor. Besides, after Fred died, Bev had decided that she didn't need another man in her life. It would be easier on her emotions if she could learn to manage on her own. Of course, the absence of romantic love had left a huge void in her life.

Dan walked Leona to the front door, glancing at Bev as he passed. She averted her gaze and tried to concentrate on the price stickers in front of her.

"See you soon, Danny," Leona said, reaching for the doorknob. The door swung open before she could turn the knob, and in walked Ellis Hampton with a large box.

"I've brought the train," he announced.

Glad for the interruption, Bev pushed her chair away from the desk. "Oh good. I'm happy you came by today, Ellis."

"I'm sorry it took me so long to get the engine repaired, but I ran into a few problems," he apologized.

"That's all right. Let's get it set up under the tree in the display window." Bev was almost at Ellis's side when Leona took a step backward. The two women collided, and Leona collapsed on the floor.

Chapter 10

"Are you all right?" Dan knelt next to Leona, who appeared to be more embarrassed than anything else.

"I–I'm fine," she stammered, "but I think the heel of my shoe is broken." She pulled off her shoe and held it up for his inspection.

"Yep. The heel's almost off." He helped Leona to her feet. "Maybe I can put some glue on it to help hold it together until you can get the shoe properly repaired."

She glared at Bev. "This is all your fault. If you hadn't gotten in my way, I never would have fallen."

Bev's cheeks were pink, and she looked visibly shaken. "I—I'm sorry, but I wasn't expecting you to step backward."

Leona's face contorted. "So now it's my fault?"

"I didn't say that. I just meant—"

Dan stepped between the two women. "It was only an accident, but if it will make you feel better, Leona, I'll pay for the repair of your shoe."

"Thank you, Danny. I appreciate that." She batted her eyelashes at him.

"I'm glad you weren't hurt, and I'm sorry we bumped into each other." Bev reached her hand out to Leona, but the woman moved quickly away. She turned with a shrug and followed Ellis to the window display, where Amy was decorating the tree.

Leona removed her other shoe and handed it to Dan. "It might be a good idea if you check this one over, too."

He led the way to his studio and, once they were inside, motioned to the chair beside his desk. "Have a seat, and I'll see if I can find some glue."

Leona dropped into the chair with a groan.

"That woman you hired is sure a pain."

Dan looked up from the desk drawer he was rummaging through. "What's that supposed to mean?"

"When I first came into the store, she wouldn't even let me talk to you. Said something about you being on the phone. Then after I told her I was going to your studio anyway, she tried to stop me." Leona frowned. "I think she's jealous because I'm prettier than she is. That's probably why she tripped me."

Dan blew out a ragged breath. "I'm sure she wasn't trying to trip you, Leona. Bev's a nice lady."

"How would you know that? She's only been working for you a short time."

He squeezed a layer of glue onto the broken heel and gave no reply.

"Are you dating the woman? Is that why you've been giving me the brush-off lately?"

He squinted. "What? No!"

She smiled. "That's good news, because I wouldn't like it if you were interested in some

other woman. I think we—"

Dan handed her the shoe. "Here. I believe this will hold until you get home."

"Thanks."

He leaned forward with both elbows on his desk. "Leona, I think I need to clarify a few things."

She blinked and gave him another charming smile. "What things?"

He cleared his throat, searching for words that wouldn't sound hurtful. "I'm not completely over my wife's death yet, so there's no chance of me becoming romantically interested in anyone right now."

Leona opened her mouth, but he held up his hand. "Please, hear me out."

She clamped her lips tightly together and sat there with her arms folded.

Dan reached inside another drawer and retrieved his Bible. When he placed it on the desk, she frowned. "What's that for?"

"I'm a Christian, Leona. I believe God sent His Son to die for my sins."

She shook her head. "Oh no, Danny. You're too

nice to have ever sinned."

"That's not true. Romans 3:23 says, 'For all have sinned, and come short of the glory of God.'"

"Are you saying that includes me? Do you think I'm a sinner, Danny?"

"We all are," he answered. "Everyone needs to find forgiveness for his or her sins, and the only way is through Jesus Christ."

"I'll have you know I did a lot of volunteer work during the war, in addition to my nursing duties," she said with a huff. "I've always tried to be a good person, so I don't need anyone telling me I'm a sinner."

"I'm sorry you feel that way."

Leona wrinkled her nose. "And I don't see what any of this has to do with you and me developing a relationship." She relaxed her face and reached over to touch his arm. "I can make you forget about the pain of losing your wife if you'll give me half a chance."

"The Bible teaches that those who believe in

Jesus should not be unequally yoked with unbelievers, Leona. So even if I were ready to begin a relationship, it would have to be with a woman who believes in Christ as I do."

Her face flamed. "You mean because I don't go to church and rub elbows with a bunch of hypocrites, I'm not good enough for you?"

"That's not what I'm saying."

"What, then?"

Lord, help me, Dan prayed. His fingers traced the cover of the Bible. "As a Christian, I know it wouldn't be right to date someone who doesn't share my beliefs."

"What about that woman you spent Thanksgiving with?"

"What about her?"

"Does she go to church and believe in the same religious things as you?"

Dan closed his eyes as a mental picture of Bev flashed into his mind. She was a Christian, and as near as he could tell, she lived like one. Ever since he'd first met Bev, he'd been attracted to her sweet, caring disposition. She reminded him of Darcy in so many ways. He rubbed the bridge of his nose. *If that's so, then why can't I—*

Leona shook his arm, and Dan's eyes popped open. "Are you ignoring me?"

"No, but I. . ."

She pursed her lips. "I want to know one thing before I go."

"What's that?"

"If you have no interest in me, then why have you been leading me on?"

Dan cringed. Had he led Leona on? He'd thought he was being kind and neighborly when he'd agreed to have dinner with her a few times. He was only trying to set a Christian example.

"If I led you on, I'm sorry," he said.

Leona stood and pushed her chair aside with such force it nearly toppled to the floor. She grabbed her shoes and tromped across the room, but before she reached the door, she whirled around. "Just so you know—you're not the only fish in the Atlantic Ocean. When you turned me down for Thanksgiving dinner, I invited an old army buddy of my husband's over, and he was more than willing to share the meal with me."

Dan was about to comment when she added, "I'll send you the bill for the shoe repairs!" The door clicked shut, and Leona was gone.

Dan leaned forward and continued to rub the pulsating spot on his forehead. *I never should have had dinner with her.* When he glanced at the picture of Darcy, he thought of Bev again, and feelings of confusion swirled around in his brain like a frightening hurricane.

"Come look at what I found, Mommy!" Amy called to Bev.

Several minutes ago, the child had become bored with decorating the tree and had wandered over to a box of stuffed toys that had recently been donated to Twice Loved.

"I'm busy, honey. Can it wait awhile?" Bev asked over her shoulder. She and Ellis were still trying to get the train set up.

"That's okay. I can manage on my own if you need to see what your daughter wants," Ellis said with a grin. "I've got six grandkids, and I know how it is when one of 'em gets excited about something."

Bev smiled gratefully. "Thanks. I'll be back soon." She stepped across the room and knelt on the floor beside Amy. "Let's see what you've found."

Amy lifted a bedraggled-looking teddy bear from the box and gave it a hug. "He reminds me of Uncle Dan."

Bev tipped her head and studied the bear. One eye was missing, both paws were torn, the blue ribbon around its neck was faded, and some of the fur on the bear's stomach was gone. He didn't look anything like Dan, who was always nicely dressed, with his hair combed just right.

"What is there about the bear that makes you think of Dan?" Bev asked her daughter.

"He needs someone to fix him, Mommy," Amy said in a serious tone. "I think he's lonely and has no one to love." She pointed to the bear. "Can we take him home so he won't be sad?"

Bev's eyes stung with unshed tears. She didn't know why she felt like crying. Was it the touching scene with Amy and the bear, or did she feel sorry for herself because, like the tattered bear, she too was lonely and needed love? Was it possible that Dan felt that way?

"I'll tell you what," Bev said, giving Amy's arm a gentle squeeze. "If you promise to help me finish decorating the tree in the window, I'll see about buying that bear for you."

"Can he go home with us today?"

"Yes. After I patch him up."

"Okay, but I would love the bear just the way he is."

Bev smiled. "That's how Jesus sees us, and the best part is that He loves us the way we are." She held out her hand. "Should we go back to the window and finish the tree now?"

Amy nodded and grabbed the bear by one torn paw. "Until we're ready to go home, I'm gonna put him in the window with the dolls and stuffed toys. That way he can see all the people who walk by the store."

As Bev started across the room, the door to Dan's photography studio opened. Leona marched through the toy store with a pained expression.

Bev was tempted to say something, but the woman's angry glare made her decide to keep quiet.

A few seconds after Leona stormed out of the store, Dan emerged from his studio, wearing his coat, hat, and a pair of gloves. He looked upset, too. Was he mad at Bev for bumping into his girlfriend? Did he think she had done it on purpose?

"I'm sorry, but something's come up and I won't be able to help you today after all." He nodded at Bev.

"I'm sure I can manage."

He was almost to the door when he halted. "Uh—can we take a rain check on that dinner I promised you and Amy?"

She swallowed around the lump in her throat. "Sure. It's probably best if we don't go out anyway."

Dan merely shrugged and opened the door.

He's probably going after Leona. Bev reached into the cardboard box and removed the train's caboose. She was on the verge of tears. What had happened between yesterday's pleasant Thanksgiving dinner and today? *It must be Leona Howard.*

At that moment, Bev made a decision. From this point on, there would be no more romps in the snow or friendly dinners. Her relationship with her boss must be kept strictly business.

Chapter 11

Holding tightly to Amy's hand, Bev trudged up the stairs to her apartment. Today was Thursday, and her workweek was nearly finished. The last two weeks had been the hardest she had experienced since Dan hired her to run Twice Loved. Not only had there been more customers than usual, but despite her best intentions, she continued to struggle with her feelings for Dan. He seemed sweet and attentive where Amy was concerned, even allowing her to visit his photography studio a couple of times. He'd also taken the child Christmas shopping one afternoon, which gave Bev the freedom to wait on customers without any distractions. Around Bev, however, Dan was distant and appeared to be preoccupied. He'd been friendly and attentive until the day after Thanksgiving, and Bev didn't know what had happened to change things.

She'd thought at first that Dan's lack of interest in her was due to Leona Howard, but shortly after the woman's last visit to the store, Dan had told Bev he had informed Leona he wasn't free to pursue a relationship with her because she wasn't a Christian. He'd also made it clear that he hadn't fully recovered from his wife's death and didn't know if he would ever be ready for a relationship with another woman.

Bev opened the door to her apartment, allowing her thoughts to return to the present. She and Amy had purchased a Christmas tree at a reduced price, and the man at the tree lot would be delivering it soon. For the rest of the evening, she planned for the two of them to decorate the tree, snack on popcorn and apple cider, and sing whatever Christmas songs were played on the radio.

That should take my mind off Dan Fisher, Bev told

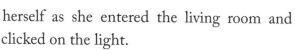

herself as she entered the living room and clicked on the light.

Amy went straight to her room and returned a few minutes later with Baby Sue. She placed the doll on the sofa and plunked down beside her. "We're gonna wait right here till the tree arrives," she announced.

"I think it's here already, because I hear the rumbling of a truck."

Amy jumped up and raced for the door. Bev caught her hand, and the two of them hurried down the steps and onto the sidewalk.

The delivery man was already unloading the tree from the back of his pickup. "Want me to haul this upstairs for you?"

Bev shook her head. "I'm sure I can manage."

"It's a pretty big tree, ma'am."

"Thanks anyway."

He merely shrugged and climbed back into his truck.

Grabbing hold of the cumbersome tree trunk and directing Amy to go ahead of her, Bev huffed

and puffed her way up the flight of stairs until she stood in front of her door. She leaned the tree against the wall and studied it, wondering if the oversize tree could be squeezed through the doorway.

She turned to Amy. "Sweetie, I want you to go into the living room and wait for me. After I bring the tree inside, we can begin decorating it."

"Okay."

Amy disappeared inside, and Bev grabbed hold of the tree, lining the trunk up with the door. She gave it a hefty thrust, but it only went halfway and wedged against the doorjamb. "*Oomph!*" She pushed hard again, almost losing her balance and catching herself before she fell into the scraggly branches.

Bev dropped to her knees and crawled under the limbs. *Maybe I can grab hold of the trunk and push it through that way.* Grasping both sides, she gritted her teeth and gave it a shove. The tree didn't budge.

With a sense of determination, Bev reassessed her situation. This time, facing the hallway, she would back in under the branches, grab hold, and

try to pull the tree as she scooted through the doorway.

Bev had backed partway through the evergreen tunnel when a pair of men's shoes appeared. She froze.

The branches above her head parted, and Dan grinned down at her. "Oops. Looks like I'm too late."

"Too late for what?"

"I. . .uh. . .brought you a tree."

"You did what?"

He shuffled his feet a few times, and Bev pushed against the branches of the tree again, hoping to dislodge it. In the process, her hair stuck to a prickly bough. "I'm trapped, and so is the tree," she admitted sheepishly.

Dan reached through and untangled her hair. "See if you can back your way into the living room, and I'll try to follow with the tree."

Bev was skeptical but did as he suggested. Once she had clambered out from under the branches, she stood off to one side and waited to see what would happen.

To her amazement, Dan and the tree made their entrance a few minutes later. He obviously had more strength than she did.

After Amy greeted "Uncle Dan," Bev asked the child to go to her room and play. Then she turned to face Dan. "Now what's this about you bringing another tree?"

He swiped his hand across his damp forehead. "I—I figured you probably couldn't afford to buy a nice tree, so I bought you one and was going to leave it outside your door."

"An anonymous gift?"

He nodded and offered her a sheepish grin. "To be perfectly honest, I've done a couple other secret things, too."

She frowned. "Such as?"

He pointed to the front door. "While I wasn't the one who actually hung the wreath there, I did pay for it and asked the girls from church to put it on your door Thanksgiving morning."

Bev sank onto the couch. "Anything else I should know?"

He shifted uneasily. "Well. . ."

She blew out an exasperated breath.

"I know the man who owns this building, and when you said you were interested in renting an apartment here but might not be able to afford it, I agreed to pay your landlord the extra twenty dollars he normally would have charged per month."

Bev's mouth fell open. "Why would you do such a thing without asking me?"

"When I offered to increase your wages, you flatly refused, and several times you've mentioned that you don't want any charity. I thought the only way I could help was to do it anonymously."

Bev's body trembled as she fought for control. How dare this man go behind her back! "Please take the tree and the wreath to your own home. I'll speak to Mr. Dawson in the morning about the rent."

"Does that mean you won't accept any of my gifts?"

She shook her head as tears pooled in her eyes.

"I'm sorry if I've offended you, Bev."

She made no reply.

"I—I'd better get going." Dan turned for the door. "I hope I'll see you at the store tomorrow."

As much as she was tempted to quit working at Twice Loved, Bev knew it would be difficult to find another job. Besides, she enjoyed the work she did there. "I'll make sure I'm on time," she mumbled.

The following morning, Bev found it difficult to concentrate on her work. Last night, she and Amy had decorated their tree, and she'd lain awake for hours thinking about Dan and the gifts he'd given her in secret. She had lost her temper and hadn't shown any appreciation for his thoughtfulness. *I need to apologize, but he also has to understand that I won't accept his charity.*

She glanced around the store. Christmas was only a few days away, and most of the toys had been picked over. Most that were left needed repair. She'd been too busy with customers to get more mending done. She was also behind on the book work and wanted to finish that before the week was out. It was time to get busy and quit thinking about Dan.

Since there were no customers at the moment, Bev decided to start with the book work. She seated herself at the desk, opened the drawer, and reached for the ledger, prepared to record the previous day's receipts.

Near the back of the drawer, she discovered a folded slip of paper. Funny, she'd never noticed it before. Curious, she unfolded the paper and silently read the words.

One thing I have learned since I was diagnosed with leukemia is not to worry about things I can't change. Every day God gives me is like a special gift, and I am putting my trust in Him. I've also learned to accept help whenever it's offered. I used to be too proud to ask for assistance, thinking I could do everything in my own strength. But since I became sick, I have no choice except to rely on others. Dan has been especially helpful, often setting his own needs aside for mine. I know he would rather be in

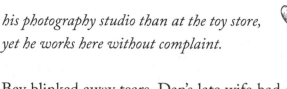

his photography studio than at the toy store, yet he works here without complaint.

Bev blinked away tears. Dan's late wife had obviously written the note before she'd become too ill to be at the store, but for whom was it intended? Perhaps it was a letter to a friend or family member and Darcy had forgotten to mail it.

The poor woman had been through more than Bev could imagine, yet Bev realized Darcy had kept a positive, thankful attitude despite her ill health. She'd learned not to worry and had been willing to accept help, two areas in which Bev often struggled.

She realized, too, that Dan had only been trying to help when he'd given money toward her rent and purchased the tree and wreath. Even so, she didn't want to feel beholden to a man who only saw her as his employee—a man who was still in love with his wife and might never be ready for a relationship with another woman. Too bad she hadn't been able to keep from falling in love with him.

Dan stared at Darcy's Bible lying on his desk. He'd discovered it in the bottom drawer of their dresser this morning and felt compelled to bring it to work with him. Maybe it was because Christmas was fast approaching and he needed the comfort of having something near that belonged to his wife. This was Darcy's favorite time of the year, and every Christmas carol he heard on the radio, every decorated tree he saw in a window, and each Christmas shopper who came into the toy store reminded him of her.

Dan leaned forward and closed his eyes. *Help me, Lord. Help me not to forget my sweet Darcy.*

He had been fighting his attraction to Bev ever since she came into the store looking for a doll for her daughter, yet he hadn't succumbed to the temptation of telling her how he felt. He couldn't. It wouldn't be fair to his wife's memory.

Dan opened his eyes and randomly turned the pages of Darcy's Bible. To his surprise, an envelope fell out, and he saw that it was addressed to him.

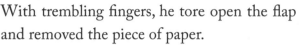

With trembling fingers, he tore open the flap and removed the piece of paper.

> *My Dearest Dan,*
>   *If you're reading this letter, then I have passed from this world into the next. One thing you can be sure of is that I'm no longer in pain. Take comfort in knowing I am healed and in my Savior's arms.*

Dan's throat constricted as he tried to imagine his precious wife running through the streets of heaven, whole and at peace. With a need to know what else she had written, he read on.

> *My greatest concern is that you will continue to grieve after I'm gone, when you should be moving on with your life. You're a wonderful Christian man who has so much love and compassion to give. Please don't spend excessive time mourning for me. Praise God that I'm happy, and ask Him to bring joy into your life again.*

Just as you and I have shared the love of Jesus with others, I pray you will continue to do the same—not only through what we've done at Twice Loved but in your personal relationships.

It's my prayer that God will bring you a special Christian lady, because I know you will be the same wonderful husband to her as you have been to me.

As you know, I always wanted to give you children, and I pray the Lord will bless you and your new wife with a family. Please know that by loving and being loved in return you will be honoring my wishes.

May God richly bless you in the days to come.

All my love,
Darcy

Tears welled up in Dan's eyes and spilled onto his cheeks. Darcy's letter was like healing balm, given at just the right time. He realized now that

Darcy wanted him to be happy and to find love again. But could he find it with Bev? Was she the one God meant for him? If so, then he had some fences to mend.

Dan reached for the telephone. "First things first."

"*Family Life Magazine*," a woman answered on the second ring.

"May I speak to Pete Mackey?"

"One moment, please, and I'll see if he's in."

There was a brief pause, then, "Mackey here."

"Pete, this is Dan Fisher, with Fisher Photography."

"Ah yes, I remember. How are you, Dan?"

"I'm doing okay. Listen, Pete, I was wondering if you're still interested in interviewing me for that article you're writing on grief."

"Sure am. When can we talk?"

"I'll give you a call right after the New Year. How does that sound?"

"Great! Thanks, Dan. I'm glad you've changed your mind."

Dan smiled. "Actually, it was my late wife who changed my mind, but I'll tell you about that during the interview."

"Okay. I'll look forward to hearing from you."

Dan hung up the phone feeling as if a heavy weight had been lifted from his shoulders. Now he had one more hurdle to jump, and that *couldn't* wait until after the New Year. He pushed his chair away from the desk and headed down the hall for Twice Loved.

When he entered the store, he realized Bev was with a customer. He paused inside the door, waiting for her to finish wrapping a doll for an elderly gentleman. As soon as the man left, Dan stepped up to her. "If you have a minute, I'd like to speak with you."

She tipped her head. "Is something wrong?"

"Not unless you—"

The telephone rang, interrupting him.

"I'd better get that." Bev moved to the desk and picked up the receiver. "Twice Loved. May I help you?" Her face paled, and Dan felt immediate

concern. "Thank you for letting me know. I'll be right there."

"What's wrong?" he asked when she hung up the phone.

Bev turned to face him, her eyes pooling with tears. "That was Amy's teacher. Amy fell from a swing during recess and has been taken to the hospital."

Chapter 12

Bev paced the floor of the hospital waiting room, anxious for some word on her daughter's condition.

"You're going to wear a hole in the linoleum. Please come sit beside me and try to relax," Dan said, patting the chair next to him.

She clenched her fingers and continued to walk back and forth in front of the window. "What if her leg's broken or she has a concussion? What if—"

Dan left his seat and came to stand beside her. "Whatever is wrong, we'll get through it together."

We? After the way I spoke to him last night, why is Dan being so nice? And what does he mean when he says "we"? Bev glanced at him out of the corner of her eye.

"It's going to be okay," he said with the voice of assurance. "Amy's a tough little girl, and she's got youth on her side."

Bev nodded slowly. "I know, but—"

"But you're her mother, and you have a tendency to worry."

"Yes."

"I understand, but worry won't change a thing." He took Bev's hand and led her over to the chairs. "Let's pray, shall we?"

Bev glanced around the room. There was an elderly couple sitting across from them, but they seemed to be engrossed in their magazines. "You want to pray now?"

Dan offered her a reassuring smile. "Absolutely." In a quiet voice, he prayed, "Heavenly Father, we ask You to be with Amy and calm her if she's frightened. Give the doctors wisdom in their diagnosis, and help Bev remember to cast her burdens on You, the Great Physician."

Bev thought of a verse of scripture from the book of Matthew she had read the other evening. "*'Take therefore no thought for the morrow: for the morrow shall take thought for the things of itself.'*"

Lately, she'd been trying not to worry so much, but staying calm was hard to do when something went wrong. Especially when that "something" concerned her daughter.

A few minutes later, a nurse entered the room and called to Bev. "The tests are done, and you may see your daughter now."

"Are her injuries serious?" Bev tried to keep her voice calm, but her insides churned like an eggbeater.

"The doctor will give you the details," the nurse replied, "but Amy's going to be fine."

Bev drew in a deep breath. *Thank You, Jesus.* She turned to Dan. "Would you like to come with me?"

He nodded and took her hand.

Dan stood at the foot of Amy's bed, relief flooding his soul. Her leg wasn't broken, but her ankle had been badly sprained. She did have a concussion, though it was thought to be mild. The doctor wanted to keep her overnight for observation.

Bev sat in the chair beside Amy, holding her hand and murmuring words of comfort. It was a touching scene, and Dan felt like an intruder.

Maybe I should leave the two of them alone.

He turned toward the door, but Amy called out to him. "Where ya goin', Uncle Dan?"

"To the waiting room so you and your mother can talk."

Amy looked over at Bev. "We want Uncle Dan here, don't we, Mommy?"

Bev nodded. "If he wants to be."

Dan rushed to the side of the bed and stood behind Bev's chair. "Of course I want to be. I want. . ." What exactly did he want? Was it to marry Bev and help her raise Amy? He rubbed the bridge of his nose. No, it was too soon for that. They'd only known each other a few months.

"Can you come to our place for Christmas

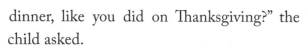

dinner, like you did on Thanksgiving?" the child asked.

Dan's gaze went to Bev, seeking her approval—or at least hoping for a clue as to whether she wanted him there or not.

She smiled. "I'm sorry for the unkind things I said when you stopped by our place with the tree."

"It's okay. I understand."

"No. I was wrong to refuse your help and the offer of gifts, and I hope you'll accept my apology."

"Only if you will accept mine for overstepping my boundaries."

She nodded. "If you have no other plans for Christmas, we'd love to have you join us."

He shook his head. "I don't think coming to your place is a good idea."

Tears welled up in Amy's eyes, and her lower lip trembled. "Why not? We had fun on Thanksgiving, didn't we, Uncle Dan?"

Dan felt immediate regret for his poor choice of words. Leaning over the bed, he took the child's other hand. "I had a wonderful time on Thanksgiving. It was the best day I've had in a long time."

"Then why won't you come for Christmas?" This question came from Bev, whose vivid blue eyes were full of questions.

He smiled. "Because I'd like to have you and Amy over to my house for Christmas dinner."

Bev's mouth dropped open. "You're planning to cook the meal?"

He shrugged. "Sure, why not?"

Amy giggled. "Can ya make pumpkin pies?"

Dan grinned then winked at Bev. "Actually, I was hoping you might furnish the pies, but I can roast the turkey and fix the rest of the dinner."

Bev's expression was dubious at first, but she gave him a nod. "It's a deal."

Dan had been rushing around for hours, checking on the bird he'd put in the oven early that morning, peeling and cutting the potatoes and carrots he planned to boil later on and placing presents under the tree. He wanted everything to be perfect for Bev and Amy. Though they might not realize it, they had brought joy into his life, and they deserved to have a special Christmas.

Satisfied that everything was finally ready, Dan put the potatoes in a kettle of cold water, grabbed his coat and gloves, and headed out the door. It was time to pick up his dinner guests.

A short time later, he stood in front of Bev's door, glad she hadn't refused his offer of a ride. It would have been difficult for her and Amy to catch the bus, what with the child's ankle still slightly swollen, not to mention the weather, which had recently deepened the snow on the ground.

When Bev opened the door and smiled at Dan, it nearly took his breath away. She wore a lilac-colored gown with a wide neckline and a skirt that dropped just below her knees. And this time she had on a pair of hose. "You're beautiful," he murmured.

"Thanks. You look pretty handsome yourself."

He glanced at his navy-blue slacks and matching blazer. Nothing out of the ordinary, but if she thought he looked handsome, that was all right by him.

Bev opened the door wider. "Come in and I'll get our coats and gifts."

Dan stepped into the living room and spotted Amy sitting on the sofa, dressed in a frilly pink dress that matched her flushed cheeks.

"Hey, cutie. Ready to go?"

She nodded and grinned up at him. "I can't wait to give you my present, Uncle Dan."

He leaned over and scooped the child into his arms. "And I can't wait to receive it."

"That was a delicious meal," Bev said, amazed at how well Dan could cook. She was also surprised at the change that had come over him since Amy's accident. He'd driven Bev to the hospital and stayed with her until they knew Amy was okay. He had taken her home, back to the hospital the next day, and given them a ride to their apartment when Amy was released. Now, as they sat in Dan's living room inside his cozy brick home on the north end of town, Bev could honestly say she felt joy celebrating this Christmas.

"I'm glad you enjoyed dinner and equally glad I didn't burn anything." Dan nodded at Amy, who sat on the floor in front of the crackling fire he'd built earlier. "How about it, little one? Are you ready to open your presents?"

Amy scooted closer to the Christmas tree. "Yes!"

"Okay then. Who wants the first gift?"

"Me! Me!"

Dan chuckled and handed Amy a box. "I believe this one's from your mother."

Amy looked at Bev, and she nodded. "Go ahead and open it."

The child quickly tore off the wrapping, and when she lifted the lid and removed a delicate bisque doll, she squealed with delight. "She's beautiful, Mommy! Thank you!"

"You're welcome, sweetheart."

Amy smiled at Dan. "Can I give Mommy her present from me now?"

"Sure." Dan pointed to a small package wrapped in red paper. "It's that one."

Amy handed the gift to her mother and leaned against Dan's knee as Bev opened it.

"This is wonderful!" Bev exclaimed, as she held up a framed picture of Amy sitting on the patchwork quilt Dan's late wife had made. "How did you do this without me knowing?"

"When you were busy with customers, I took Amy into my photography studio and snapped her picture," Dan answered. "We bought the frame the day I took her Christmas shopping."

Bev kissed Amy's cheek and was tempted to do the same to Dan, but she caught herself in time. "Thank you both. I appreciate the picture and will find the right place to hang it when we go home."

"Here's my gift to you, Amy." Dan placed a large box in front of the child and helped her undo the flaps. Inside was a quilt—the same quilt that used to hang in Twice Loved and he'd used as a background for Amy's portrait.

Amy lifted the colorful covering and buried her

face in it. "I love it, Uncle Dan. Thank you."

"It's a precious gift, Dan," Bev said, "but don't you think you should give the quilt to a family member?"

Dan took Bev's hand. "That's what I have in mind, all right."

Bev's heartbeat picked up speed. What exactly was he saying?

Dan reached into his jacket pocket and pulled out a flat green velvet box. He handed it to Bev with a smile.

She lifted the lid and gasped at the lovely gold locket inside. "It's beautiful. Thank you, Dan."

"Open the locket," he prompted.

She did—and soon discovered there was a picture of Amy on one side and a picture of Dan on the other.

"I'm in love with you, Bev," Dan said, as he leaned over and kissed her.

Bev's eyes filled with tears, and at first she could only nod in reply. When she finally found her voice, she whispered, "I love you, too."

Amy grinned from ear to ear then handed Dan a large gift wrapped in green paper. "Here, Uncle Dan. This is for you, from me and Mommy."

Dan tore open the wrapping and lifted a brown teddy bear from the box. It had new eyes, patched paws, a pretty blue ribbon around its neck, and a sign on the front of its stomach that read: I AM TWICE LOVED.

He tipped his head in question, and Bev smiled in response. "It was Amy's idea."

Dan gave Amy a hug then lifted Bev's chin with his thumb. He kissed her once more and murmured, "I believe God brought the three of us together, and just like this bear and the quilt I gave Amy, we have been twice loved."

"This is the Christmas that a war-weary world has prayed for through long and awful years. With peace come joy and gladness. The gloom of the war years fades as once more we light the National Community Christmas Tree."—President Harry S. Truman, National Tree Lighting Ceremony, December 24, 1945.

The attack on Pearl Harbor on December 7, 1941, and subsequent entry into World War II made many Americans fearful that Christmas would not be joyfully celebrated again for a long time. But on December 24, 1941, with Winston Churchill, who was in town for the Arcadia Conference, by his side, President Roosevelt did go ahead and light the national Christmas tree on the lawn of the White House. Over 20,000 Americans attended the celebration.

Then from 1942 through 1944, the national

Christmas tree was erected on the South Lawn and decorated, but it was not lit due to both the need to conserve electricity and to black out Washington from any potential nighttime air raids.

With the surrender of Germany in May and Japan in September of 1945, Americans once again had liberty to celebrate special holidays. But Christmas 1945 remained a sad time for those who had lost loved ones in the war and those waiting for word on the missing. Still there was renewed hope as troops were returning home and the war effort had pulled the country out of the Great Depression into a new era of prosperity. President Truman encouraged the country to take time to celebrate Christmas with goodwill toward all men and to look ahead to a time of peace.

For further reading see the Harry S. Truman years at www.whitehousechristmascards.com or *Christmas 1945: The Story of the Greatest Celebration in American History* by Matthew Litt (2010).

Wartime Recipes

Home-front cooks during World War II were restricted on what they could fix to eat by what food rations they were allowed to buy. Meat, sugar, butter, and cheese were the most commonly rationed items, but later they included processed and canned foods and any imported foods like coffee. Backyard gardening and animal husbandry were encouraged to help provide a family what the grocery stores could not. Often recipes of the time were aimed at ways to make a little stretch into a filling dish.

Creamed Chipped Beef on Toast

This preserved meat recipe became a staple in army mess halls and soon made its way to home-front kitchens. Spam was another canned meat that could be used in place of the beef.

2 tablespoons butter or bacon grease
1 (4 ounce) package of chipped beef (can be rinsed to reduce the salt), chopped or shredded

2 tablespoons flour
2 cups milk
pepper

Melt butter in saucepan over medium heat. Add beef, stirring to coat in butter. Add flour, stirring to coat beef, and cook for about 5 minutes. Slowly add milk, stirring continuously as it comes to a boil and thickens. Pepper to taste. Serve over toast.

Rivel Soup

2 cups flour
½ teaspoon salt
1 egg, beaten
6 cups chicken broth
Shredded cooked chicken, optional

Combine flour and salt with egg, until mixture is crumbly. Bring broth to boil. Sprinkle in mixture crumbles. Reduce heat and cook 10 to 15 minutes. Add chicken during last five minutes of cooking if desired.

Escalloped Corn and Oysters

4 tablespoons butter
4 tablespoons flour
2 cups milk
2 tablespoons green pepper, chopped
2 cups canned corn
1 (8 ounce) can oysters, drained
2 eggs, well beaten
1 cup cracker crumbs
1 teaspoon salt
Pepper to taste
Buttered bread crumbs
Shredded cheese

Melt butter in saucepan; add flour. Stir over medium heat until flour is bubbly and lightly browned. Slowly add milk and stir until bubbly and thickened. Remove from heat. Add green pepper, corn, oysters, and eggs. Stir until well blended then add crackers and seasoning. Pour into buttered casserole dish. Top with buttered bread crumbs and cheese. Bake for 30 minute at 350 degrees.

Candied Apples

5–6 cups water
5 ounces cinnamon imperial candies
2–3 drops red food coloring
8 apples, pared and halved

Bring water, candies, and food coloring to boil in large heavy kettle. Place apples in syrup. Cook, turning only once. Add more candies as you cook apples. Judge readiness by color of apples. They should also be fork tender but not mushy. Cook one floating layer of apples at a time. Boil remaining syrup down to jelly—ready when it fills the prongs of a cold fork. Pour some jelly over apples. Store remainder of jelly in glass jar for later use on bread and butter. Serves 8–16.

Honey Rice

¾ cup honey
½ cup raisins
2 cups white rice, cooked
1 tablespoon butter
1 tablespoon lemon juice

1 teaspoon vanilla
¼ cup chopped nuts, optional
Cinnamon

In saucepan over medium heat, heat honey then add raisins and rice. Pour into shallow buttered dish. Dot with butter. Bake 20 to 30 minutes at 350 degrees until golden brown. Transfer to bowl and mix in lemon juice and vanilla. Sprinkle with nuts and cinnamon before serving.

Ration Cake

No egg, no milk, no butter, no problem as long as you still had some sugar rations left.

1 cup water
1 cup sugar
½ cup lard or shortening
1 cup raisins
½ teaspoon salt
1 teaspoon cinnamon
1 teaspoon nutmeg

1 teaspoon allspice
¼ teaspoon ground cloves
1 ¾ cups flour
1 teaspoon baking soda
Chopped nuts, optional
Candied fruits, optional

In saucepan over medium high heat, combine water, sugar, shortening, raisins, salt, cinnamon, nutmeg, allspice, and cloves. Bring gently to boil and continue boiling for 5 minutes. Remove from heat and let cool. Sift in flour and baking soda, stirring only until combined. Add nuts and fruit. Place in greased 9-inch square pan. Bake for 20 minutes at 350 degrees.

Wacky Sheet Cake

½ cup butter or margarine
1 cup water
½ cup lard or shortening
4 tablespoons cocoa
2 cups flour
2 cups sugar

1 teaspoon salt
1 teaspoon cinnamon, optional
2 eggs
½ cup milk
1 teaspoon baking soda
1 tablespoon vinegar or lemon juice

In saucepan, bring to boil margarine, water, shortening, and cocoa. Sift together flour, sugar, salt, and cinnamon. Combine dry mix with liquid. Add eggs one at a time. Mix in milk, soda, and vinegar. Place in greased 9 x 13-inch pan. Bake 15 to 20 minutes at 350 degrees.

Buttermilk Pie

1 cup sugar
3 egg yolks
2 teaspoons butter or margarine
1 tablespoon vinegar
1 teaspoon cinnamon
2 heaping tablespoons flour
1 ½ cups buttermilk

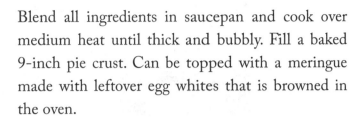

Blend all ingredients in saucepan and cook over medium heat until thick and bubbly. Fill a baked 9-inch pie crust. Can be topped with a meringue made with leftover egg whites that is browned in the oven.

Faked Whipped Cream

An option for when you were out of rations for dairy products.

2 egg whites
½ cup powdered sugar
1 cup apple, grated
1 teaspoon lemon juice or vanilla

Beat egg whites until stiff. Slowly add half the sugar while beating. Then add grated apple and the rest of sugar, alternately while continuing to beat. Quickly stir in lemon juice. Serve on cakes, pudding, and the like.

Frugal Craft

Stuffed Camel

In a few easy steps, you can create a cute stuffed camel toy. This pattern was inspired by Rag Bag Toys, a 1940s-era booklet with patterns to create cost-conscious, homemade toys during the thrifty war years. Use spare scraps of fabric or worn-out clothing for the body of your camel. For stuffing in a pinch, try cotton cosmetic balls—just pull the fibers apart and fluff before stuffing.

Materials—
Remnant fabric (about ¼ yd)
Thread
Embroidery floss
Stuffing

Instructions—

1. Enlarge pattern to ¼ inch larger than desired finished size. (Sample toy is 9 inches tall.)
2. Fold fabric in half, wrong sides together, and cut using pattern.
3. Sew two fabric pieces with right sides together, leaving small opening at belly.
4. Turn right side out.
5. Using embroidery floss, embellish as desired. Add eyes, eyelashes, mouth, hooves, etc. Braid three lengths of floss together, knot at one end, and tack in place for tail.
6. Stuff.
7. Whipstitch opening closed.

Wanda E. Brunstetter is a best-selling author who enjoys writing Amish-themed, as well as historical, novels. Descended from Anabaptists herself, Wanda became deeply interested in the Plain People when she married her husband, Richard who grew up in a Mennonite church in Pennsylvania. Wanda and her husband live in Washington State, but take every opportunity to visit their Amish friends in various communities across the country, gathering further information about the Amish way of life.

Wanda and her husband have two grown children and six grandchildren. In her spare time, Wanda enjoys photography, ventriloquism, gardening, reading, beach-combing, and having fun with her family.

In addition to her novels, Wanda has written Amish cookbooks, Amish devotionals, several Amish children's books, as well as numerous novellas, stories, articles, poems, and puppet scripts.

Visit Wanda's Web site at www.wandabrunstetter .com.